A
MOST
UNUSUAL
UMBRELLA

ELAYNE REISS-WEIMANN
RITA FRIEDMAN

NEW DIMENSIONS IN EDUCATION, INC.
50 EXECUTIVE BLVD.
ELMSFORD, NY 10523

Printed in U.S.A.

ISBN 0-89796-999-5

1 2 3 4 5 6 7 8 9 SPC 8 9 8

12406 (Hardcover)
12521 (Softcover)

One day, posters are placed throughout
Letter People Land.
The posters say, "Please be at the
Town Square tomorrow.
A new Letter Person will arrive in a most unusual way."

1

Uncle Ulver telephones the mayor.
"Who is the new Letter Person?" he asks.
"Her name is Miss U," answers the mayor.
"Is she really arriving in a most unusual way?"
asks Uncle Ulver.
"Oh yes," says the mayor, "Miss U is arriving
by umbrella."

3

"Arriving by umbrella!" repeats Uncle Ulver.
"That is a most unusual way."
"Miss U's umbrella has a small computer,"
explains the mayor.
"The computer helps Miss U land her
most unusual umbrella."
"Is it dangerous?" asks Uncle Ulver.
"Oh, no!" says the mayor.
"You don't ever have to worry about Miss U."
"It is all most unusual, most unusual,"
says Uncle Ulver in amazement.
"I will be at the Town Square to welcome Miss U."

Uncle Ulver tells everyone about Miss U
and her most unusual umbrella.
Everyone is very excited.
"We have never seen an umbrella with its own
computer," they say.
Some people make welcoming signs for Miss U.
Others make welcoming banners.
Uncle Ulver prepares welcoming balloons.
The marching band practices welcoming music.

Early Monday morning, people gather at
the Town Square to welcome Miss U.
The popcorn man sets up his popcorn machine.
The woman who sells hamburgers sets up her stand.
"We are ready to welcome Miss U," says Uncle Ulver.
"You are a wonderful welcoming group," says the mayor.
"You will make Miss U very happy."

Everyone waits and waits for Miss U to arrive.
Suddenly, Uncle Ulver shouts,
"Look up! Look up high!
I see an umbrella."
Everyone looks up, up, up.
"Yes, yes," they say excitedly, "we can see
an umbrella."
As they watch, the unusual umbrella comes
closer and closer.

"Here comes Miss U," says the mayor happily.
"Please, hold up your welcoming signs and banners.
Start playing your welcoming music.
Let the welcoming balloons fly."
Before anyone can do as the mayor asks, a most
unusual thing happens.
The unusual umbrella stops in midair.
Then, instead of landing, it goes up, up, up, and away.

13

"Miss U come back," shouts Uncle Ulver.
"Please land.
We are waiting to welcome you."
Miss U presses key after key on the computer,
but the unusual umbrella keeps going up, up, up.
Miss U holds the umbrella handle tightly as she
checks the computer.
"Something is wrong with the computer," she says.
"But I will try to land again."

Miss U presses different keys on the computer.

The unusual umbrella starts to move down.

Soon, Miss U is over the Town Square.

Again, the unusual umbrella stops in midair.

But it will not land.

This time, it starts to move away from the Town Square.

"Miss U, you are passing the Town Square," shouts
Uncle Ulver.

"Please come back.

We are waiting to welcome you."

17

"The computer is not working," shouts Miss U.
"I cannot make this unusual umbrella land
at the Town Square.
I will have to land somewhere else."
"Land anywhere!" shouts Uncle Ulver.
"We want you safely on the ground.
We will run after you.
We will welcome you wherever you land."
"Hurry, hurry!" says Uncle Ulver to all the people.
"Run after Miss U.
We must be sure she is safe, and we must welcome her."

WELCOME

19

Quickly, people grab the signs, banners, balloons, popcorn, hamburgers, and band instruments.
Then, they all run after the unusual umbrella.
The unusual umbrella stops in midair over an open field.
Miss U waves to everyone.
"See, I am absolutely safe," she says.
"I will try to land here."
Miss U presses several keys on the computer.
Suddenly, the most unusual thing of all happens.

WELCOME

POPCORN

21

The unusual umbrella gets wider and wider and wider.
"I see an unidentified flying object," says
Uncle Ulver in a very worried voice.
"Do not worry," says Miss U.
"It is only I, Miss U, with a most unusual umbrella."
"Please land, Miss U," pleads Uncle Ulver.
"I cannot help worrying about you."

WELCOME

23

"There is no reason to worry," says Miss U.
"I will land.
Sometimes it takes me a little longer."
Miss U presses many keys on the computer.
This time, the unusual umbrella gets
narrower and narrower.
At last, it looks like an umbrella again.
But instead of landing, it goes up, up, up.
The people put down the signs and banners.
The band stops playing.
Uncle Ulver holds onto his balloons.
"It is not easy to welcome Miss U," he sighs.

Miss U checks the computer again.

"The computer needs a new part," she thinks.

"I do not have a spare part with me.

I cannot make the umbrella land, but there is

a way I can land."

Miss U presses keys on the computer.

The unusual umbrella starts to move down.

"Look up!" shouts Uncle Ulver.

"There, over the Town Square.

It is Miss U again.

Hurry, hurry! Run to the Town Square.

We must be there to welcome Miss U."

"Here we go again," sigh the people,

shaking their heads.

People run to the Town Square carrying
signs, banners, balloons, popcorn, hamburgers, and
band instruments.
Once again, the unusual umbrella stops in midair.
"The unusual umbrella will not land," says Miss U.
"But I will land."
"Don't jump," says Uncle Ulver.
"You are up too high."
"I will not jump," says Miss U.
"I will slide."
"Slide?" repeat the people in confusion.
"Watch and listen," says Miss U.
She presses key after key on the computer.
The unusual umbrella does not move.
Then, all of a sudden, the umbrella handle gets
longer and longer and longer.
At last, the handle touches the ground.

29

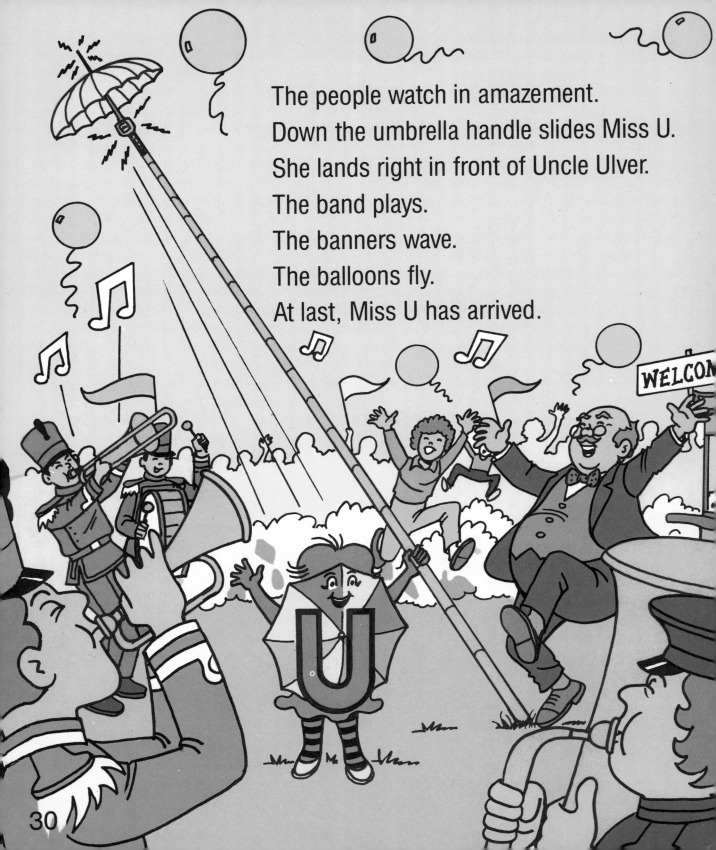

The people watch in amazement.
Down the umbrella handle slides Miss U.
She lands right in front of Uncle Ulver.
The band plays.
The banners wave.
The balloons fly.
At last, Miss U has arrived.